SHANNON

ALSO BY CAMPBELL MCGRATH

Seven Notebooks (2008)

Pax Atomica (2004)

Florida Poems (2002)

Road Atlas (1999)

Spring Comes to Chicago (1996)

American Noise (1993)

Capitalism (1990)

SHANNON

———

a poem of the

LEWIS AND CLARK EXPEDITION

CAMPBELL MCGRATH

ecco

An Imprint of HarperCollins Publishers

SHANNON. Copyright © 2009 by Campbell McGrath. All rights reserved. Printed in the
United States of America. No part of this book may be used or reproduced in any manner
whatsoever without written permission except in the case of brief quotations embodied in
critical articles and reviews. For information, address HarperCollins Publishers, 10 East
53rd Street, New York, NY 10022.

HarperCollins books may be purchased for educational, business, or sales promotional
use. For information, please write: Special Markets Department, HarperCollins Publishers,
10 East 53rd Street, New York, NY 10022.

FIRST EDITION

Designed by Mary Austin Speaker

Library of Congress Cataloging-in-Publication Data
McGrath, Campbell
Shannon: a poem of the Lewis and Clark Expedition / Campbell McGrath.—1st ed.
p. cm.
ISBN: 978-0-06-166129-7
1. Lewis and Clark Expedition (1804–1806)—Poetry. I. Title.
PS3563.C3658S53 2009
811'.54—dc22   2008036866

09   10   11   12   13   ID/RRD   10   9   8   7   6   5   4   3   2   1

For Sam

ACKNOWLEDGMENTS

———

WITH THANKS TO: Florida International University and Philip and Patricia Frost for enabling the research and writing of this poem; the many writers who have preceded my own exploration of this (or similar) terrain, including (but not limited to) Maurice Manning, Frank X. Walker, Stephen Ambrose, Robert Penn Warren, Mark Twain, Francis Parkman, Meriwether Lewis, and William Clark; the editors of *The Meadow*; the rangers of Niobrara State Park; and my family for listening to the first draft of this poem as we navigated the back roads of Knox and Boyd Counties, Nebraska, and Gregory, Lyman, and Charles Mix Counties, South Dakota.

CONTENTS

———

Lewis and Clark

August 26, 1804

After jerking the meat killed yesterday and preparing the elk skins for a tow-rope we set out, leaving Shannon and Drouillard to hunt for the horses lost last night. Directed them to follow us, keeping on the high lands.

Proceeded on. Passed a cliff of white & dark blue earth of 2 miles extent on the left shore and camped on a sand bar opposite the old village called Petite Arc. A small creek falls into the river 15 yds wide below the village on the same side. This village was built by an Indian Chief of the Maha nation by the name of Petite Arc (or Little Bow), displeased with the Great Chief of that nation (Black Bird). He separated with 200 men and built a village at this place. After his death the two villages joined together again.

Appointed Patrick Gass Sergeant in place of Sergeant Floyd, deceased.

Great quantities of grapes, plums of three kinds, 2 yellow, one of which is larger and one longer, and a 3rd kind round & red. All well-flavored, particularly the yellow sort.

—William Clark,
Captain, Corps of Discovery

This morning the morning star much larger than common. Drouillard came up and informed that he could neither find Shannon nor the horses. He had walked all night. We sent Shields and J. Fields back to look for Shannon & the horses, with directions to keep on the hills to the Grand Calumet above the Niobrara River.

We set sail under a gentle breeze from the S.E. At 7 miles passed a white clay marl or chalk bluff. This bluff is extensive. Beneath it we discovered stone resembling limestone encrusted with a glassy substance I took to be cobalt ore. Three miles above this bluff we set the prairie on fire, to let the Sioux know we wished to see them.

At two o'clock an Indian swam to the pirogue, we landed & two others came. They were boys. They informed us that the Sioux were camped near. One Maha boy informed us his nation was gone to make peace with the Pawnee.

We sent Sergeant Pryor & a Frenchman with the Interpreter Mr. Dorion to the camp to invite their Great Chiefs to a council at the Calumet Bluffs.

We proceeded on 1 1/2 miles farther and camped on the starboard shore.

—WILLIAM CLARK,
CAPTAIN, CORPS OF DISCOVERY

SHANNON

1.

It is a fine & open country in every aspect hereabouts.

The very prairie, grasslands, thickets

Or brakes along the several streams with elk

& deer largely therein.

Of those legendary buffalo first sighted

& shot by J. Fields this week, alas

None discovered by me as yet this day or last

Whilst tracking runaway horses.

Those two did flee as if unwilling ever to be caught

But I came upon them at evening yesterday

Drinking water in a sandy draw

Well-trampled by hoof-marks dark as bruises

Sure evidence of buffalo in great plenty.

In the event the fugitives appeared

Not unhappy at sight of me.

Found their hobble ropes trailing

Which I did retie forcefully

Pleased as I am by this outcome.

It was my hope to recover these horses

& so demonstrate my worth

In such regard to the Capts. generally—

I do not misdoubt them, only certain statements

Overheard among the company concerning

My youth & stature as a hunter, which I deem false.

Last time I did kill an elk buck yet R. Fields

Brought in five deer to top it. So it was
I importuned the Capts. to set me this errand
Those Fields Brothers having done so
Previously, nor did I aim to disappoint them.
Why should youth count against a man
In this Missouri country?
Eighteen & years in the backwoods
I am a better hunter than most back home
& this a newer land
Nor Capt. Lewis nor Clark
Hoary greybeards
Yet Pres. Jefferson saw fit to appoint them
Command of this Expedition. Well
It is done
& the horses recovered at any rate
By myself alone.

Pres. Jefferson is a man much admired
By Capt. Lewis, who frequently
Recounts his love of the same hills Capt. Lewis knew
As a boy in Virginia, rambling long days
Outdoors, the joy of which I share in kind.
Says they much resemble the country
Along the Ohio River, yet
These lands along the Missouri

That much starker, bolder, gouged
& abandoned to grass & sky.
As God much imbues this world with his Self
I guess now the Capts. are
In these parts, & us, & Pres. Jefferson.
Like to which the moonlight
Enumerating each stalk with blue shadows.
These wild, wind-torn lands flung to the horizon
Will soon enough be states
Of the Union
Why else fashion a Corps of Discovery?
If such they become
I would hope to name one
New Ohio.

Coming on evening I make shift to camp
Shy of the river one final night
& will welcome sight of it & my companions
On the morrow. These horses will not stray.
I have tied them to a cottonwood tree
Not trusting the hobbles. What I took to be stones
In the gloaming were skulls of buffalo.

2.

Fair-set, windless, fine & warm.
Clouds at dawn resembling raked embers
Now diminished, nor any wisp to be seen.
Having never conceived a sky
So grand as this I wonder
If the Western Ocean truly resembles
The accounts
Capt. Lewis has given
Could it be larger still? How might such fact
Be ascertained as scientific certainty?
Maps may well declare it so
Yet the Capts. would no doubt contrive
Something to measure it by.

Continuing north & west towards the river
Crossing small streams
Thick with pestering mosquitoes
It being somewhat marshy, much sign
Of beaver, muskrat, otter
Along all these creeks & rivers.
We could make hay
In these parts
& not with farming but I mean—furs.
Not to mention the buffalo, those
Dusty hides must be fit for some use back east.

The Indians do rely upon them
& I am eager to sight
One of those shaggy fellows.
Having seen somewhat of their skill
With bow & arrow
Would much appreciate to view as well
The Indians' way of hunting them on horseback—
In the villages of the Otos & the Mahas
Many braves were absent
Hunting buffalo, & the squaws busy
Preparing the hides variously
But I do not anticipate to meet with friendly tribes
Hereabouts. At home rough treatment
Would be my expectation
Caught alone by the Shawnee or Wyandot
On their treaty lands, extending still
As far west as the Wabash in Indiana Territory.
I do not believe these so-called Sioux
Or Dakota
Likely to be kinder.

Kickapoo, Osage, Missouri, Oto, Maha
Or Omaha—the Expedition has already met
More Indians than I ever witnessed
& the Capts. on the lookout still for the Ponca

Kansas, Arikara, Hidatsa, Mandan, Minataree—
Tribes further west known by rumor alone
As Blackfeet, Piegan, Atsina, Crow &c.

Myself as well keep vigil for any such
& happy to have gained
The high bluffs that mark the river
& my point of rendezvous.

Well now, here is my journey's end
Withheld awhile it seems.

I have found the Missouri River
Just as I left it
But not my companions
The Capts. & the Corps of Discovery
Having passed this point already
As proved by sign of a pirogue having landed
On this shore, many footprints
Somewhat obscured but certain in their inference.
Again do I regret not obtaining provisions
Of Drouillard when we split our search party
Happy as I was to be shed of him
He being a master tracker & I so eager
For sole glory. More & more

It seems mere vanity
& yet none for it now but to search out pawpaws
& berries along the river.
These two days I have eaten all I carried
Some handfuls of jerky & no more.
The fellows will make sport of me
O but breakfast will taste fine in camp tomorrow
Even if only cornmeal & suet
Better yet venison or bear steaks.

Nor should I complain, it ill suits me.
Were he here my Father would say
Nothing wrong with hunger
George my boy
If it steel a man's resolve.

Which assuredly it has.
Come sunup I aim to lead these horses
Upriver fast as ever they did ramble.

Soldier on, George my boy, soldier on.

3.

Curse myself for stupidity

Curse my aim wasting balls on such as these

Horned-goats or antelope-deer

Even more curse the makers of this rifle

Curse the state & foundry & gunsmith alike

For it don't fire true & I am hungry.

Nor would I choose to aim at such

Fleet & flighty game

They resembling less deer than startled birds

To my mind, veering & jumping

Astoundingly into the high grass

But that Capt. Lewis

Much desires one for his specimens

& to report such discoveries to Pres. Jefferson.

More vanity. It is the poor workman

That blames his tools

George my boy

So my Father would say, & rightly.

What most vexes me is this.

Not setting out to hunt but to track fool horses

In my excitement I did not trouble

Refilling my pouch with shot

To discover it contained but five balls

Only after firing twice at antelope

Which is pure foolishness.

Shot one large ball at an elk
Feeding on alder bark
Missing altogether
& one to kill a fair-sized deer for supper
& to breakfast upon the morrow.
Which leaves but one remaining.
Though my horn be full of powder
What use is it without bullets?

Following the bluffs still hopeful
Of sighting my companions before sundown
Beheld an island of white pelicans
Diving for their supper
In golden, sun-gilt water with great uproar.
Had I a hook I might fish as well
In any stream—at the village of the Mahas
We caught 800-odd fish
With seines & drag-nets made of willow branches
Such as pike, bass, salmon-trout, perch
Red horse, buffalo fish & some
Curious white catfish resembling small dolphins.
Plus which abundant shrimp Capt. Lewis declared
As fine tasting as in New Orleans.
Yet if I dawdled at every creek
Along the Missouri River

I would never catch up to the Expedition
Such is my quandary.

Set the horses to graze in pasture there
Well roped & secured.
I am troubled to light a fire
Lest it be the Sioux
That take it as a signal before the Expedition
Yet I must cook my meat for dinner.
Rain this afternoon.
Such was my vantage from those bluffs
To track the showers yawing
Across the plains
As black-curtained sailing craft.
Some buffalo likewise, the first
I have seen, at great distance.
If it were to hunt I had come
& so equipped
Might have pursued those beasts freely
Across an undisturbed range for many miles.

This night clearer, lightning flashing
Eastward on the horizon
Alone & the stars otherwise brightly manifest.
Though I have obtained no mastery

My attendance upon Capt. Lewis
Has showed me much of the sextant's use
& those stars relevant to lunary calculation
By name Antares, Altair, Regulus
Spica, Pollux, Aldebaran, Formalhaut
Arieties, Alphe & Alplo Pegas.
Some number of which I now descry
Taking comfort to imagine Capt. Lewis
Engaged in similar observation this very hour.

The Capts. set much store in measuring
With sextant & chronometer
Thereby to chart the river's course
Via longitude & latitude, plus
Mapping these newly acquired territories
As desired by Pres. Jefferson—
Hills, islands, width of rivers, &c.
Especially tributaries which enter from the north
Are of interest, as by treaty
This Louisiana Territory contains
All lands that drain into the Missouri River
West to the Stony or Rocky Mountains
Whereby Capt. Lewis does hope to discover
Some far-wandering stream that might trespass
North beyond the 49th meridian

So gaining access
To those western lands of British Canada
Even up to the Saskatchewan River.
Often do the British poach our furs
From the Illinois Country, the Western Reserve, &c
Which it would give the Capts. pleasure
To return the favor.

Dog-tired from driving the horses all day
The brown one especially
Being contrary and prone to lurch & stumble
Yet is my sleep postponed
By these prolific showers of shooting stars
Blazing their luminary trails across the heavens.
Much is writ in their countenance
But not the destiny of men or such trifles.

4.

At sunrise I made shift to mark a likely copse

& shot a deer—to my surprise

It ran over a mile up the draw & away

Across broken country before falling though it were not

A bad shot. Being my last bullet

I had no recourse

But to track it, fearing the horses to escape

All the while in my absence. I eagerly endeavored

To dig the ball free

But it was irrecoverable having struck bone

As yesterday that other flew clear & gone

Alas. This deer was black-tailed

& exceedingly large, resembling an elk

Somewhat in size & appearance.

Haunches, saddle, liver—took all

I might to sustain me

Perchance the Expedition has got farther ahead

Than I have willingly contemplated.

I do not believe Capt. Lewis

Would leave any man behind

Nor Capt. Clark equally would forsake me.

The Corps of Discovery is a body of men

Both loyal & true

In my opinion, notwithstanding the sad loss

Of Sgt. Floyd. Yet they are sworn

To persevere in their great task

Which one man's fate cannot gainsay.

Not a single hour ought I to have tarried

In hopes of spying a buffalo

But there is no help for it now.

Curse these horses

To move so we might catch up

They are the very source of my consternation.

Git on, horse

Git on.

Capt. Lewis has noted the names

Of many new plants

Not seen even in green Kentucky

Such as that Evening Star which flowers

Fragrantly at sunset in profusion hereabouts

Several prairie-clovers

These buffalo grasses tall as a horse

& yucca gloriosa. Curious

It a spiked, raw, blue-throated thing

Glory being known along the Ohio River

As magnificent & lordly

The throne of God, pearls & fire, &c.

Have made a poultice of skunk grass & mud
Such as Drouillard showed the use of
& salved it on the withers
Of the brown horse
Where it got incised by some old spur
Of a dead tree down the bank
In one ravine.
Much dust & trouble
In those gulleys
Which intersect the river at every draw
Or the banks sheered away in flood
Steep, rocky & oft-times impassable.
I will make shift to keep to the prairie tomorrow
Minding the Missouri only to catch
Sight of the Expedition.
It would not do
To pass them by oblivious.

Why else I am eager to rejoin my fellows
Beyond the chance of Indians
& hunger
Is this—Moses Reed.

Last week he did attempt
To run off to the village of the Otos

For which the Capts.

Might have shot him for desertion

We being officially enlisted in the U.S. Army

As Pvts. for the most part

But were lenient.

Four times he ran the gantlet

We with fists & switches

To show the nature of our disregard

For his turpitude in our ranks.

What I fear is not

Such blows

But Reed's disgrace, he being

Discharged from the Corps of Discovery

& considered like to a servant

Among us now

To be sent back with the pirogue

To St. Louis come winter.

I do not misdoubt my character

& that of my family

Is well-known to Capt. Lewis in particular

Nor his charity of opinion

Still I would make haste

To reassure him of my whereabouts
& intention.

That same evening among the Otos
Were Capt. Lewis' birthday
Which to celebrate
He did dispense an extra gill of whiskey
To each man, a sentiment we honored in turn
With fiddle music & songs & dancing
Long past midnight, thinking no more upon
That scoundrel Moses Reed.

5.

Fog on the river thick as goose down.

Now it lifts, swirling clear for a moment

Ripples & channels, then lost

Again to whiteness

All that glinting river vanished, gone.

As like to a dream have I wakened or the light

Might be facet of some other place

One might reside

As when we set out to hunt as boys

Coming over a ridge

Did see a white stag in the meadow there

Among hills in Kentucky.

Shot to no avail.

Though I was among the best shot

In that country miles around considered.

Truth to tell I wished to miss him

But did not say so

To my Father & brothers beside me.

Burning-off, the fog

Lifting.

Small herds

Of elk coming out from the arroyo

To silver water & shadows

Of clouds over the same hills & wind

Amongst the grasses grown

Ceaseless now.

Buffalo in large numbers

Crossing the sandy channel of a river

Entering the Missouri

Broadest tributary I have observed since the Platte.

Here too in the braiding of ways a pattern

Of barest impression

As might be stained by steady use upon some tool

Or implement, my rifle stock

Curse which, tool unsuited to any purpose

In my plight

Or axe, shovel, pick

As even the pew of the church

Beneath my Mother's touch grew

Dark-stained by her devotion

Knee & hand alike

So worn, polished, oiled, grooved.

Though it was not in truth an older church

Or congregation & the wood-work

Inexpert in my regard.

That pastor had been sold a bill of goods

But anyway it stood

Alright & the grain of it

I recall as richly as the rushing grasses

Or the wash of Mother's hair

More favorably than his sermons, rain clouds
I never much believed
Fit the skies along the Ohio.
Often as I might I passed my Sundays hunting
Which my Mother did not approve.
Contrived to leave out from home
& not return
Until that bell had tolled
Its final hullabaloo.

Buffalo—in the darkness
Before dawn I heard their bellow
& tremble of their footsteps
Coming within some 20 yards of where I lay.
That I had wished but days past
To sight a single creature seems sheer whimsy
Now they are revealed in such numbers
As cannot be reckoned.

This brown horse will not answer
Any longer—it is lame
& that cut grievous despite the balm.
No doubt I have driven it too hard
Still it does hinder me
In my pursuit. I have no bullet

Yet must be rid of it come what may
& so decide to cut him loose
Before crossing this subsidiary river
Which has proven wide and shallow at its juncture
Running near parallel from the west
To join the Missouri at the base of these
Stout hills & bluffs.
I suppose the wolves will have him
But no help for it.

One time only I beheld any sight
Alike to that white stag.
Three days south from the Ohio River we had ridden
Into the bluegrass plateau of Kentucky.
In all that high country spring
Was not yet come
But abundant in suggestion, first buds
On the laurel & cherry
Sap running in the shag bark hickory
We tapped for syrup
& when I came through the sugar bush
Following sign of a large buck
Beheld the shape of the thing exactly
As a revelation
In the form of an angel

Robed entire in white flowers or

Prophet or ghost

Or burning bush I feared

To approach, falling even to my knees

But in the end determined

It was a dogwood tree come early to blossom.

That was a true & terrible fear

& near as I ever came

Or will come to believing.

Nor did I mention it to Parson Macready

Foreknowing his sanctimony

As I did not believe it was

The Son of God

But something other—perhaps

The flower of which Jesus even was made

If such be possible. A flower

That stood before Him, or stands behind Him

Surrounding the idea of Him

Like the sun haloed behind that cloud.

A garment of numinous blossoms

Upon everything equally is what I mean.

Not a portent such as Parson Macready

Would testify but a sign

Of spring come early to flower

Is all.

& plenty.
I am neither a wise nor aged man
But my eyes & my sense agree
Together on the nature of most things—
Why would I require
Holy doctrine to discriminate?

Afterward my Father did tease me
George my boy
We shall make a preacher of you yet
& my brothers Thomas & John
Shaking most every dogwood branch
South of the Ohio River
Three days riding home saying, Lo, George
Be it man or angel
Come before you now?

It were neither, Thomas.

Were but a tree
In flower.

Might that it should comfort you
In my stead, dearest John
Where you rest.

6.

This morning climbed a large round hillock
Set back some half-mile or so
From the river bluffs, wishing to rise above
& scout the country
For sign of the Expedition ahead
& possibly to recognize once & for all
The location of these Great Rocky Mountains
Long promised. Some days ago
At the Village of the Maha we made shift
Along with Capt. Lewis to climb
Another such hill, atop which the burial mound
Of their great chieftain, Blackbird
Interred upright upon his horse.
There we did tie our flag
As tribute & sign of friendship to that nation.
They are much reduced by the small pox
The Maha, & set upon
In said weakness by their fellows.
Worse luck that Capt. Lewis did intend
To inoculate these Indians against it
Only to find the vaccine spoiled in transit—
Pres. Jefferson is much concerned
With the pox & would vanquish it.
Nonetheless the Capts. did honor
To their chieftains & big men with such articles

As breech clouts, tobacco, flags, &c.
Being somewhat short in trade goods
Certain certificates from Pres. Jefferson
Recognizing their friendship with the United States
Made little impression upon them.
One chief of the Otos by name Big Horse
Turned back his certificate as useless
Angering the Capts. This Big Horse
Arriving buck naked to the parlay
To demonstrate his poverty, no wonder
He might wish some more useful article
Yet he did set us howling.
It were the small pox killed Blackbird
Along with many others.
No more than three hundred of their people
Remain. From Blackbird's mound we could see
Nothing but plains across vast distances
& grass & sky
& the river shining silver.

Same silver, same river my distraction
From hunger & hundreds of brown martins
Flitting in the sunshine after insects—
This mound attracts them as files to a magnet.
Many grasshoppers much fiercer

Armored than back east, it is said the Indians
Eat them & I might yet.
Only with berries in the bottom lands
Plentiful hereabouts have I purchased
Peace with my stomach.
As raspberries, damson berries, serviceberries
Blue currants, goose berries
Huckleberries & whortle berries
Plus which the small plums or pawpaws
Sweet & fine if ripe.

More like a truce than a proper peace.
Temporary suspension
Of hostile acts.

High, craggy bluffs, betimes I detour
Along the very edge of them
Eager for their vista, despite the river twists
& turns so. Where
O where
Have the Capts. got to?
Must be driving the keel boat steady under sail
To make such time, plus which the pirogues.

Alone with the black horse now I cover
Good distance daily, they cannot
Keep ahead of me forever it would seem.

Git on, horse.

Sun something fierce, garrulous birds
& buzz of the grasshoppers
& buffalo come to drink twining & filing
Well-worn trails to the water's edge
The river wending among uncounted sand bars
With what one might call ease
Or seeming accident
Though I have been taken to wonder these days
Whether it might be some absolute purpose
Hidden there?

Why would God create a thing
That wanders aimlessly?
He would seem to prefer
Straight-thinking
If I may presume, so as to simplify
The task. Why would He

Create such an animal as these buffalo?
To feed men, which purpose they no doubt admirably
Fulfill for the Indians at any rate?

So many buffalo aggregated together, small herds
& large, a single vantage comprising many thousands
& here some lumbering up the bank like oxen
Others on a hill aways south lowing & mooning
Some ponderous bulls in rut charging & roaring
The ground shaking as with thunder
When one group rushes suddenly past my vantage
Only to merge into the larger band on the other side
Like river waters backing & swirling
Sheaves of fur & hair caught up in nettles
The dust of hooves & those rolling & lying in it
& their heaps of turds steaming everywhere
& those dried out the Indians use for kindling
& some calves sporting or frisking like lambs
Many bones in the long grass, horns & bleached skulls
Skittish packs of prairie wolves keeping watch
Various antelope, deer & elk in company
& the black-tailed mule deer abundant now.
It is a sight of no small magnificence.
These grasses, their equal abundance in the wind

Betimes I find myself floating among them
Flowing with the clouds across
The hills & herds
& within the grasses, from the hawk's height
To the dust-valley at the ant's eye
Their great Missouri a stream I might piss out
If not so damned parched.
Must make shift to the river
To fill my skins
Before nightfall. These grasses
Are like a skin
To the earth, or a quilt or blanket—no
It could only be God that had knitted such a thing
& he don't need it to keep off the chill
& such is not considered
Man's work. Being a man
I might imagine God would need a woman
For quilting, mending & plenty
Besides.

I do believe
I have tread unintended
Into the fields of blasphemy.

Who then has put such thoughts into my head
If not God Himself? Surely
Not the Devil.
I do not believe that rascal entwined
In this billowing tapestry
With nothing for him to grasp upon
But clouds & wind
Or hide behind & rear up from
Not even the yucca gloriosa
A difficult plant but not evil-intended.
Is this also blasphemous?
I believe Parson Macready would say so
But he is often off the beam
& a poor judge
Of workmen & cheap besides.

If my thoughts arise
Direct from this landscape
How other than God-ordained
Could they be?
For it is all of a piece.
Who made the grass
Made also

                    wind

        dust

                thorn
            the grasshoppers

                        shadow & light

        a dove

I wish
Would set upon that stump
To wring its neck
& eat it raw my hunger grows
Powerful.

This much for certain—if God
Did create the buffalo
He made one great, strange, daft animal.

7.

Startled awake stiff & dreaming
Upon the breasts of Constance Ebson.
Fine as they are, it disturbs me
To be tracked into this wilderness by such desires.
O what can a man do about that?
Soldier on, George my boy, soldier on.

Foraging for fruit to breakfast upon
I caught the scent of skunk—
Indeed it were a family of pole-cats there
Of which the largest raised-up its tail
At sight of me hastily withdrawing
From that thicket only to find myself
Pursued by mother pole-cat
Several hundred yards before eluding her
Unanticipated speed & determination
By leaping a small creek
And circling back to my camp
With no injury but to my pride.

Cool wind sprung up this morning
Like fall in Pennsylvania, is it
Come September yet?
Still blowing brisk & grey with rain promised
Vast flocks of birds upon the river

Set down to keep clear of the storm
Ducks, geese, certain swans, &c.
No scrap of deer meat left this afternoon
I stalked within some dozen yards
Of a swan near to shore seemingly unaware
But when I sprung the bottom proved
Abrupt & I fell into the water.
Wet through now
To spare the rain that trouble.
On several islands here again the pelicans
Whose food I might attempt to steal
Or nests to rob
But the current is fleet.
It were a poor idea & a peril to drown.

One time my brother Thomas killed a swan.
Swifts gathered up from the fallow
Hayfield downhill like idle chatter.
In the woods my brother shot the swan—
Why did it go in there, among such a darkness
Of trees? Soon as he shot
The branches lifted up & scattered
Across the sky. It was a great flock of pigeons
Roosted there, branches heavy
With them in the dawn just coming.

Such hunters we were
Never to notice them huddled
Dark as apples for the taking. & then
The white feathers of that bird to contend with
In those woods, plumage of blood
All over that brilliant swan
& the pigeons chattering overhead
All morning in their passage.

Failing at the river I have determined
To fashion a bullet
From such as might come to hand
There being stones of every size & description
Fit to answer, & so fill my pouch with candidates.
I make shift to travel some mile or more south
Upon the prairie, thinking which animal
Best to make my attempt upon
When I observe myself come into a most
Remarkable situation. All about me
Upon the slope of a low rise
Small animals contrive to poke their heads
From an array of holes & tunnels
Dug thereon. Like to ground squirrels

They are, somewhat longer of body

& they do give voice

To barks or yips

Unlike any squirrel in Ohio.

Thinking this might be fair game

I loaded my rifle with the roundest river stone

In my collection, tamped & shot—

Which blast of smoke failed even to dislodge

It from the barrel, as I had feared.

A stone is not a bullet

But a stone

However you might wish it.

Next I did determine to set upon

These barking squirrels by hand, so many

There were, & so many sundry dens for them

To manifest from, nor was I

Quick enough, or patient.

One hole from which

A fellow continuously clambered in & out

I staked myself to watch, lying hidden

Just by the brow of the hill—

In all that time

He never did appear, not once.

As sentinels they were contriving to signal my presence
Like any ordinary predator to those others unseen
& I was not equipped to dig them out
& time pressed upon me, imagining each hour
The Expedition to be drawing farther ahead.

I proceeded on, until full dark
Then set rummaging among the river thickets
Again for some handfuls of grapes
& those delicious blue currants or damson berries.
No plums to be found though I searched
Even by moonlight.
Nothing to be done for it.
Wind northwest & calming after nightfall
& the rain subsiding.
My spirits somewhat subdued.
Fain to admit but I did
Despair & weep
Some while this evening.
Between my brothers & family
& now the U.S. Army for companions
I have hardly known solitude
Like this in all my eighteen years.
Night is the hardest part
& I hesitate to trust it fully.

Like walking the ice
At the edge of a pond testing
If it will bear my weight.

At the heart of my worry
Is my uncertainty—
Stated plainly, having chased the Expedition
All week unencumbered
I wonder whether per some mischance
I may have passed them by
Altogether, hidden by steep bluffs
Or river-mists
Or they delayed by some unforeseen cause
The keel boat sunk, the Sioux, &c?
Several days now I have been troubled
By the absence of signs—that is
Sure notice of the Expedition in its passage ahead.
One place along the shore were tracks
But I believe them to be Indian.
Another showed trace but had been well-trampled
By buffalo crossing there, hard to say
My skills not being precise as Drouillard & some.
Generally I believe the Capts.
In these Dakota lands may be making camp
On larger islands mid-stream for safety

Or lighting upon the far shore
By chance or preference
Nor am I able to swim over & make certain.
As I keep ambling to & from the river
It is my luck not to have hit upon
Mark of them is all—the Missouri runs
But one direction & even what skills I've got
Are fit to follow a trail this size.
If I knew I had gone wrong I would set off
Downstream this instant
To meet them, yet what if that same
Mischance were then to occur
Leaving myself going backwards and they
Forwards across the continent?
O I would be lost more completely
Than I risk to contemplate
& my hopes with nothing to seize upon
But clouds & grass, & it is my hopes
That sustain me, the idea in mind
Of that reunion more even than the fellowship.

The die is cast.

I dare not reverse my tracks,
& to sit idle

Awaiting them feels

False to my nature & to our grand purpose

Here, that being to keep moving

To forge if even blindly

Onward.

8.

Coming to the river to breakfast upon grapes & water
I spy a drowned buffalo caught up on a snag
Near shore—alas, it has gone to rot
No meat but is putrid
& unfit for a man. It was but a calf, scrawny
& well-gnawed by wolves.

In the sandy shallows all around
Schools of silverfish familiar to me as bait
From the Ohio River
But no means to net them, my shirt comes to rags
& they flee before its shadow.
I never was the fisherman to equal
My brother John, & I rue it.

My need for food assuming urgency
I set up with my collection of likely stones
To seek my rifle's determination
Once & for all
Aiming at the sandy bank from which I might
Recover any such bullet as proved feasible.
Many failed likewise to discharge
& some few flew clear
But wild & random, hither & yon
Not being fit to the barrel

Or true of shape. This practice
Leaves me
Richer in wisdom
But much reduced in powder
& the great Missouri depleted by several fistfuls
Of river-gravel.

Shining so, in the autumn sun, the river
Is like my Mother's silver necklace
Slipping across my fingers
Moving, jaunting, sparkling, restless
Coursing & entwining the many streams as one.

What if, beyond these mighty plains are plains
Even more magnificent
As this Dakota Country exceeds Ohio
In that regard, even
As heaven overshadows earth?
Just as the Ohio flows into the Mississippi
Is there beyond these plains & hills
Some consequentially greater confluence or flood
Connecting all waters, every
Least rivulet, this to that
& these to those?
Merely thinking of it I suppose it

To be true.

Or, the truth of it compels

Its image to light

Not as dream or revery

But as though the river simply existed, plain as fact

Beyond the hills of my mind, below

That horizon—as when

Another living creature near to hand

Makes its presence known in the darkness

Not by breath or motion or moonlight

But insensibly. Lest you have done it

Perhaps you cannot grasp my meaning.

But assuredly one knows he is there

Not even certain it be a foolish deer

Or my brother Thomas

Returning from his ordinary night duty.

From the Ohio River to the Missouri

I know now to be

One continuous body of water

Having traveled its course from these buffalo lands

To the great Mississippi at St. Louis

& even along the shores of the Illinois Country

& the Indiana Territory & even past

The falls of the Ohio at Louisville, Kentucky

Past the mouths of the Wabash, Kanawha, Muskingum

& even to the forks of three rivers at Fort Pitt

& the Monongahela & the Allegheny

& even into the Chartiers River in Washington County

& even into the creek behind the cabin

Nearby Claysville, Pennsylvania, where I was born.

It flows even into the Western Ocean

The Capts. will no doubt

Discover passage to—if not this river that other river

Beyond the mountains

It is the same as & one with, entire.

Settled down for the night along a grassy draw

With good berries & forage

At the foot of several rounded knolls

When smoke came clear upon the evening breeze.

At first I imagined it might signal

The cook fire of my messmates

But climbing the hill I perceived the grasses to burn

Widely on the far side of the river

Some distance removed & was much alarmed

Such fires being common practice

Among the Sioux.

Fearing myself too visible

Should any such arrive upon the opposite shore

I abandoned my chosen camp
& moved onto the prairie
& huddled there unsheltered as best I might
Feeling somewhat put-upon & vagrant.

I wish I were supplied as Capt. Lewis
With notebook paper & as gifted
Alike with Capt. Clark
Though he the less well-lettered of the two.
Capt. Lewis is a fine writer
Whose education exceeds my own
But he knows I might proceed to keep a journal
In his place if need be.
Thoughts & reflections flow through me here
Alone in these lands I may consider myself
The first American to have walked
Surely, & observations of the land generally
& such animals as I have observed.
I am no naturalist, as Pres. Jefferson would like
But I am proud to be so trusted
As a penman by the Capts.
Even if they misdoubt me somewhat
As a tracker. At any rate

Those horses they set me to find
Are lost no more.
Though I am
Curse it.
Plus which the brown horse
Become wolf-carrion.
Still it was not Drouillard
Who recovered them but me.
O sorrowful horses, where might I be
Had they not strayed?

9.

Rain strong & chilling on the plains

Draws & washes flush with runnels of rainwater

In such difficulty of travel I determine

To hunker down as best

I can contrive despite my anguish over such delay.

Titanic thunder, lightning in shorn bolts

Like cannon-fire asizzle with shivers

The hairs of my neck

The smell of it pungent as whiskey

& the wet grass likewise

In the breeze after each squall passes.

A good smell, as in a cornfield knowing

The crop were ripening well.

It was a small stand of trees

& the lee of old stumps in which I sheltered

Being those trees known as Osage Apples—

I have seen few others of their kind

Hereabouts but that copse.

Their knobby fruit is inedible but the wood

Much prized by Indians to fashion their bows

It being that strong & sturdy to work.

Which put me in mind of my failed experiments

With riverstones & so determined

To try the wood of the Osage

Not for a bow

But a bullet. Thus, taking a peg

Where a branch had set, now smooth

& pulled free as a plug of knotwood, little need

To trim it out with my knife.

Loaded same & shot from ten paces

At the stump, hurray!

It flies true but will it kill

Or wound some creature bad enough

For me to catch it?

Collecting my missile & re-loading I recalled

Those barksome squirrels

Would be the right smallness to attempt

But that was many miles backwards

Yet before any determination of what next to consider

Come fluttering two turkeys from the brush

To set below the Osage tree eating at

Fallen apples. Fair game

& did not figure to miss from such distance

Nor did I, that wooden bullet flying true

To strike tom turkey

Flush & he flapping up with a gobble

& they winging off unhurt, alas.

George my boy

Education wears many uniforms

My Father would often declare
Before setting me such tasks
As mucking out stalls &c—yes, Father
But hunger such as this
Is no lesson foreseen or desired
By either of us.

Still I have got closer
Than in many days to meat
& will persevere.

It was a fine spot upon the prairie
That Osage grove
With the storm-clouds streaming overhead
The rain grown less & the lightning
Fierce & calm by intervals.
Not turkey only but tracks of deer
& antelope collected there
& the bounding, long-eared rabbits
This country holds in plenty.
In those stumps or rambles they must den up
& so my surprise though considerable
Was lessened when that rabbit
Padded into sight
& this time my wooden bullet

Struck behind his ear & stunned him adequate
To my task & to cook up there
Contriving to light my fire rain or none
A supper such as I have never known for flavor
Of the hunger-pangs it settled.

As desired & set forth by our Father
It is my intention upon completion of this journey
To continue my proper education
At the Transylvania University in Kentucky.
All my brothers alike so intend
To study & make of ourselves what we can
In this New World. Our Father
Would not belittle whoever may choose
To remain hunters & farmers
Lord knows we have raked hay enough
Only that America
Is a land of opportunities
Best seized by those with schooling.
Himself having crossed from Ulster in Ireland
To better his station here, fine work
He made of it, raising already eight children
Plus which his service fighting
Under General Clark in the Illinois Regiment
Being Capt. Clark's elder brother

& under General Wayne at Fallen Timbers
Alongside my uncle Joseph.
My uncle Joseph was as well a veteran
Of the Continental Army
Where many times he saw General Washington
Riding camp, speaking easily
With the most common soldier among them.
This is a country of freedom
From tyranny now
& of laws, & I intend to study Law
Therefore. Must be something in it
To set us so as equals.

What would any Professor of the Law
Say about these new lands
Sovereign to us in name, whose Law
Was until recently that of Spain, & France
& now that of the United States
With no outward mark of transition?
What of the Indian nations who inhabit
This country of their forefathers?
How are they bound to such tenets?
Being outside our Law
Has done the Indians as much harm
I reckon as anything, but

I cannot see what might attract them to it.

Not from these endless buffalo prairies.

The Law does not abide in the grass

Or the plum, it does not adhere

To them as the dewdrop does.

It must be imagined.

It must be set in the mind

As the Commandments were in stone.

It must be felt, & held as true in the heart.

Yet do I not misdoubt the Indians'

Ability to so reason

They are passably fine at such

& bear greater knowledge of this land

Than any white man I ever met.

Rather, I question

Why they would trouble to.

Does the King of Spain concern himself

With our laws in his own country?

Having overthrown the King of England

Over such imposition

Do we not believe the Winnebago equally proud

& these war-like Dakota?

Still I wish the Indians would embrace it

For the Law might serve to shield them better

Than the Word of Jesus

Which relies for its vitality
Upon the goodness in men's hearts
While the Law has got
The U.S. Army to enforce it.

More years than I can calculate
Will be required to settle these plains
Yet it may be done if Pres. Jefferson so will it
& those in his office to follow.
President Lewis has a ring to it, though I concede
President Clark the more likely turn.
Lord knows they are equally intrepid men
Only Capt. Lewis somewhat philosophical
While Capt. Clark a mechanic
At heart. Which temper
Better suits the President of our nation
Is not for me to determine, only
I believe Capt. Clark
Might run an actual campaign & win it.

Well do I know what my Father
Would respond to such fancies as these.

Idleness of mind need not be wasted time
George my boy
If taken up with suitable ambition.

George my boy, if politics be the topic
Why not see fit to dream upon
President Shannon?

10.

Dreamed last night of my Father
As I have many times since leaving home.
It was a snowstorm & he fixed to go hunting
My Mother arguing against
When I discovered at the hearth
His shot pouch and powder horn
& ran carrying bullets in my hands & pockets
Seeking to track through the blizzard
A trail of footprints filling
Faster than I could follow with snow.

Set out after picking the last meat
From that rabbit & spent
Some hours this fine, cool, sunny morning
Sucking on its bones & singing out
Names of those United States
It has been my pleasure to visit or observe.

Panns-zyll-VEIN-eeah

o-HIGH-o

Cane-TUCK-hee

ver-GINN-nya

TEN-uhsee

nude-YER-zee

Indiana Territory & the Illinois
I do not include, nor any of these unsettled
Lands west of the Mississippi River.
Closest other I got to would be MAYOR-ah-lund
Passed north of on the Forbes Post Road
Bound for Philadelphia, which journey we undertook
At the desire of my Mother to visit her sister Sara
She having married a nautical merchant there.
Myself, & Thomas, & our sister Hannah
Accompanied her, being oldest
& I was much taken with the waterfront
Goods coming & going from docks & warehouses
Chandlers, ropeworks, carpentries, boatyards
Cries of the teamsters unloading vessels & trade ships
From Baltimore, Charleston, London, the Indies
Sloops & schooners, yawls & frigates
Their masts on the river like a blackened forest

Stripped of leaves by lightning fire.
Crossed the river by ferry to Camden-town
In New Jersey, & back, but never
Set my eyes upon the ocean proper, alas.

Why not sing & holler, it puts
The wolves to flight—
Last night I heard them yipping & prowling
Near to my bivouac, no doubt
Drawn to the scent of roasted rabbit
No least tidbit of which
Had I any intention of sharing.

What else I sung out was

CON-stance
EB-son
CON-stance
EB-son

O, o, o.

Like a finger
Drawing small round coins
In a frosted-over windowpane of true glass.

o mouth   o moon   o mother

How the windows at our school house
Dimmed in winter with hoar-frost
Is like the dustiness hereabouts
Dulling every leaf & blade of grass.
Mornings Thomas & I might work
A finger through it
Shaping games, paths, names, & the sun
Coming through such a tracery melted
From the heat of a fingertip
A silver to match even the Missouri River at dawn.
Those winters of schooling in Pittsburgh
I enjoyed my lessons broadly—
Basic Mathematics & some part
Of the Natural & Physical Sciences
History & Moral Law, Shakespeare & them.
Latin was not my favorite subject
But for the tales & speeches of those Romans—
Cato, that's one I recall, & Cicero
Caesar's dispatches of battles & conquests.
Those Romans were truth-talkers & prevaricators
Of a high style, sidewinding & blustering
After laws & gods, the Republic & the Empire.
I am glad we have devised

Our Constitution so as to preclude the gods
From intercession in its debates.
Ours being a singular God
While with them it was a kind of shell game
Sliding this one against that
Jupiter & Juno, Mars & Venus, &c.
The arithmetic is much simplified
With but the One
Yet there is the mystery of the Trinity
Still & other such
Miraculous calculations
& I do not like to talk unkindly but
Much of that way seems a willful blindness
Entered into, as when the farmer
Praises God for every harvest well recorded.
For where is He in that?
Does He reside in the cob
The silk, the husk?
Is He in the seed-corn
For it does multiply & bring forth?
Crops grow if well-planted, whether Christian
or Indian matters none, they
Might better thank soil & water than prayer.
Yet the Parson cries out louder, O
Who did keep the crows from the field

If not the Lord Almighty?
Has God got no better thing to do
Than playing at scarecrow?
Is He but an accountant of sheaves?
When the passenger pigeons alight & set upon
Entire districts of farms devoured
Were all them lot given over to perfidy
Equal in God's eyes? Was there
No single devout man among them?
No good wife praying for forgiveness?
It is demonstrable how much goes forward
Lacking any touch of divine investiture—
If I cast a stone in the air
It falls where it will by property
Of physical law & chance.
It might fall upon my own head
& strike me dead, would God stay that stone
Mid-air to halt it?
Which buffalo will the wolf
Eat today
Does God know?
If He is merciful why does He allow it?
If I watch a rattlesnake strike my horse
When I might have stopped it
Would you call me a wise man or a fool?

A kindly man or malicious?

What of the Wades' farm burned down

Their little baby killed?

Was that to punish Mr. Wade for drinking whiskey?

What of Mrs. Wade performing his work

Along with hers & him prone to whip her for it

& she at church each Sunday?

The God that keeps the sparrow

Keeps not the Wade baby, why is that?

Why hold an infant to account

For transgressions

It could know nothing of?

It must be to some purpose for God has willed it

& He dare not proceed by accident.

What design had He

To take my brother John from us?

To punish a childish folly of boys grown

Careless by the river?

John was the best & kindest of any

In our family, even Parson Macready acknowledged him

Such for accompanying my Mother to church

As a courtesy & we knew he was himself

Comforted there.

Nor did Thomas & I dog him for it

He was that sweet & shining.

What could the Parson offer then

To my Mother's tears in sorrow
& mine in anger
But that He moves in mysterious ways?
Any rube knows such an answer
For the palaver of a Kentucky card sharp
Caught bluffing.

This land is grown chastened
& changed somewhat
These past days
Hard traveling. Dust-ridden
Scoured & coarse
Not a tree
On the horizon all day
Only buffalo herds
Unbroken some hours keeping pace.
All these grazing creatures fed upon
The grass of these plains
Is it not strange
To believe that I might feed
A host of nations
Upon my own heart, feeling it swell so?

In a land of plenty
I travel hungry.

In a country of herds
I wander alone.

On a journey of discovery
I am the lost.

11.

This morning found a goodly grove
Of yellow paw-paws
Only to note the branches of the largest tree
Occupied by a tremendous porcupine
Engaged in eating that same fruit
Its white-tipped quills burred-out like arrows
In agitation at my arrival.
Conceiving no strategy to capture
Or dislodge the beast
I sought my breakfast elsewhere.

Mid-day came to a marsh of osier thickets
Much evidence of beaver-work
Stumps sharp as palisades
About a pond of several acres
& a beaver dam hard-made
Of mud, gravel, branches of willow & cottonwood
Nor could I break it open
Without an axe or shovel for all my imagining
Some beaver pup I might call supper.

Later I beheld an eagle strike a pigeon
From the sky in a blur of motion
Some distance away upon the prairie—
I tracked across to see perchance

The bird had fallen wounded
But a single white feather all I found.
Knowing eagle feathers to be
Highly valued by Indians for bonnets & such
I stuck it in my hat for luck & sport.

This afternoon I did observe a badger
Coming in & out of its den
In the bank of a draw overhung by reddish stone.
Watched how he preened some, scratched his claws
Dug a bit, run to the top of the bank, & down
& dug some more, gone about his business
Of being a badger generally
When some part of me began to argue
George, you are yourself
A badger.
Git on, George, act badgerish now.

It were not my Father
But a voice more curious & arcane
Causing me to wonder
Is it the hunger
Thus drawing me out of myself
Or some deeper cause?

Nor do I believe a badger

Could carry forward any such discourse.

He would not think out, Should I dig some now?

Should I hunt for food?

His way of thinking would resemble

Things & acts more purely

A conception untroubled with calculation

Such as man is consumed by.

preen   preen   preen

dig

       dig

              dig

run up the bank, scratch some

       dig
       dig
       dig

sunlight

sunlight and wind to carry

smell of grass, smell of rotted meat

food!　　food!　　food!

Some good time did pass
In which I may have been a badger—
May have believed that voice or acquiesced in its
Argument or dream-shaping
I know not which. As if
From underwater in a pond
Looking up to the sun
Tinted greenish & a reflection of yourself
Like a frog upon the under-surface
Of the water
Looking back it was.

Not unpleasant as a revery
But strange.

No, I have never
Been a frog
Or ever so considered being.

The rest of the day the country shimmers
In a haze, these buffalo

Have no fear of me

Their eyes loll & moon in the grass

& I must shout to start them from my path

& hurl a stick at one brute

Oblivious as if I were invisible

Or he aware of my absolute helplessness.

Is that orbiting hawk

The same I passed three hours hence

Or its brother? That notch in the bluffs

With boulders tumbled out

Like meal from a torn sack?

That one-horned antelope scratching its rump

On a willow stump?

Has the river left its course & I am

Rambling in circles so?

The sun just rose

Already past noon meridian

Now evening come, the stars, I don't recall

A single stone, a gully, a squirrel hole

A blade of grass—

For all my caution of drowning

In the Missouri River

It may be the vastness of this land

That consumes me.

12.

How many days my travail endures
I fail to tally properly
Arguing with myself is it 11 or 12, each morning
Blending with the last since that marvelous
Happened-upon, fine-tasting rabbit—
What luck it would be
To encounter some cousin of his today.
One voice says give up the chase
& set down at the riverside to wait
For the canoe of some trader
Loaded with beaver skins & honeycomb
Those voyageurs & trappers from St. Louis
Do traverse this stretch to the Mandan settlements
On occasion to acquire pelts
& winter coming some such might yet emerge.
But when & have I capacity
To endure? Or should I instead retreat
To the encampments of the friendly Otos & Mahas
Yet here too I misdoubt my ability
So weak have I become
On account of hunger & privation.
I feel less effectual
Than I ever recall, like a sickly child.

This morning at last I did eat
One fat grasshopper—mashed in my fist
& choked him down still kicking.

There is no salvation
In them oily bugs.

Anyhow I am so hungry as not to feel it
Heavily today, wasted to the bone
Such that my Mother ought not catch sight of me
For sake of her peace of mind. O but
She would feed me up
With bacon & bread sopped in milk.
Best not think of my poor Mother.
It sets my belly rumbling.

Very well, my decision is made
I will relent & make camp a few days here
& resume my quest if my strength might be restored.
There is a creek rich with berries
& I will seek meat however possible.
Amid the heavy creek-side canes I may shelter
As well from prying Indians

Plus the herds of buffalo which have come
To imperil my waking & dreaming hours alike.

Truth be told I cannot abide the thought
To surrender my place in the company of this Expedition
Even should death be the price for perseverance.
Surely this Voyage of Discovery outstrips
Any in our nation's history
& the Capts. our greatest explorers
since Daniel Boone.
To be among the first
To tread these newly-acquired Territories
& more to come, how I would regret
The chance of returning
With such tales
As should delight my Father & brothers
They sharing equally the honor of my enlistment.

It was my fortune to sign on with Capt. Lewis
That winter in Pittsburgh along with John Colter
Rumor having run along the Ohio
Of the Capts. & their Expedition
& all likely men aspiring to it.
My brother Thomas being one year younger
My Mother did deny him

To accompany me—I hope he may not
Hold it against me still. Come April my Father
Waved me away in the flat boat
For Louisville saying, George my boy
Scholarship is a noble ideal
Yet soldiering a fit profession for a young man
To prove his mettle the meantime.
Gave me his hunting knife
As well to sail with
It being of Spanish make acquired in Belfast
In his youth.

Honor & glory are fit reward
For this grand adventure in service to our nation
Yet we are promised 320 acres for each man
Beyond my salary as Pvt. in the U.S. Army
& Pres. Jefferson we believe
May far surpass such in his largesse
Should we succeed in our project.
Being first to spy the lay of the country
It is to be hoped we might
Choose such land as we see fit
Though far from certain.
My uncle Joseph & many veterans with him
Believed themselves due similar

Bounty lands along the Scioto River in Ohio
Yet the scrip for it proved worthless
Else the jobbers & speculators
Had procured the best land leaving none
But sloughs & hilltops
For those desiring to farm there.
He sold off his claim for a pittance
& come back down to Pennsylvania.
As a man schooled in the Law
I believe it would accrue to my advantage
In such instances, there is money
To be made in a land office hereabouts
Or I am a simpleton.
I might plat a fine city today
Along this very creek
& name it Shannontown, or Maryville
In honor of my Mother.

It might seem a solid year
Yet no more than three months have passed
Since we encountered Daniel Boone's settlement
Near the town of La Charette upriver from St. Louis
Stopping to trade for butter & corn
From his sons & cousins & other Kentuckians
He had brought into Missouri

To settle the land, but Boone himself gone
Hunting that day, alas—
I had desired to meet the man.

Would I barter my Father's knife
For some ears of corn
Though it mean more to me than anything
I have owned?

O yes.

I would trade it for a single egg
To suck from the shell
& count myself lucky in the bargain.

13.

let there be light upon the prairie dust

light & the germ of it
within the dewdrop infused, parched light
of the moon reflected constellations

pearl on yucca, immortal diamond
crown of thorns & stars

is the day come, are the stars come down
has the river fallen, John?

silver of frost & birds' eggs
rising up the first bell-stroke of light
my cloak of light to keep you

take this sword of light, this ruin

is it a dream of loneliness that calls me?

not dawn or alone, not dawn this river

far-off two-note whistle of bird-song
high-low, not alone in the silence
not alone, breathing, eyes in the night

to keep me—Pollux, Regulus, Aldebaran

is the day come, brother John?
are the stars come down to keep me, Thomas?

dewdrop, the source, fog of breath
& the river of light widening towards sunrise
this astonishment of grass, this extravagance

animals in the darkness all around me

huffing & lowing of the buffalo
sound of their lungs steaming into the light
I am not alone in the darkness

buffalo

                                        buffalo
                buffalo

        buffalo buffalo

                        buffalo

still dark but not alone, the great herds
pulsing all around me in the darkness

snort & exhalation, stomp & low

herds of buffalo breathing all around me

beards of saliva, tongue & forelock
rustle in the grass of the buffalo gathering
heavy stamp of hooves & bodies of the buffalo
fur thick with burrs of brome & sedge grass

trumpet & bellow of the buffalo herds at dawn

roar & grunt in the horn-light glinting

hump-rumble, herd wallow, gruff in the darkness
buffalo breathing in the dawn all around me
smell of the buffalo strong on the river breeze
black eyes wide as the Western Ocean
great herds of the buffalo all around me

       buffalo

  buffalo

  buffalo

                    buffalo

            buffalobuffalobuffalo

                            buffalo   buffalo buffalo
buffalobuffalo
            buffalobuffalo   buffalo
            buffalo buffalobuffalobuffalo

                    buffalobuffalobuffalo
buffalobuffalo   buffalo buffalo buffalo
            buffalobuffalobuffalo buffalo buffalobuffalobuffalobuffalobuffalo
buffalo   buffalobuffalo   buffalo
                                    buffalo
        buffalo
            buffalo buffalo
                buffalo
            buffalobuffalo buffalo   buffalo
                                            buffalo
                        buffalo
                            buffalo   buffalobuffalo
buffalo buffalobuffalobuffalobuffalobuffalobuffalo
            buffalobuffalo   buffalobuffalobuffalo

buffalo buffalobuffalobuffalobuffalobuffalobuffalo
buffalobuffalobuffalobuffalobuffalobuffalobuffalobuffalobuffalobuffalobuffal
obuffalobuffalobuffalobuffalo

buffalobuffalobuffalo

buffalo
buffalobuffalobuffalo   buffalo
buffalobuffalobuffalo   buffalo

buffalo

buffalo buffalo

buffalo

buffalo   buffalo buffalo

buffalo

buffalobuffalo   buffalo

buffalobuffalobuffalo   buffalo

buffalo

buffalobuffalobuffalobuffalobuffalo

buffalo

buffalo   buffalo

buffalo

buffalobuffalobuffalo   buffalo

buffalo

buffalo

buffalobuffalo

                                    buffalobuffalo
                                              buffalo

                                              buffalo

herds & eyes all around me in the darkness
buffalo in the dawn-light breathing
whispering, I am the buffalo-god

I am the buffalo-god, behold my kingdom

14.

At some remove in a boggy section upcreek
Stands the nest of a sea-eagle
Forked in a dead basswood tree. No eggs
& no sign of its tenant
Yet I took up from beneath it
Several heads of fish rotted through
Not to eat but as bait, my determination being
To lure some other bird to it
Upon a flat rock I had spied
With ample room to secret myself beneath
As in a hunter's blind.
In the eventuality it was a sound plan
& likely of success had I hit upon it
When my strength allowed.
Was a buzzard settled there unguessing
My presence & I jumping out
Pitiably dizzy at the effort to grasp not even
One feather, he not bothering to fly
But hopping out of reach
As if mockingly to determine might I not make
A better meal than this meager carrion?
Not this day but soon, I fear
Too soon. Exhausted I lay down
Somewhat later to dream of Constance
Tickling my arm, shoulder, neck

Then coming awake to find myself
Swarmed all over by ants, a multitude of ants
Parading across my body & for what?
Curious creatures to choose for food
Such as has none himself
Nor the least crumb upon me
Nor but grapes past ripe to eat days running.
Plus a large bush with some raspberries
The bears had left me yesterday.
Abundant bear-tracks along my little creek
Must be a den near to hand
I should by wary of it—perhaps I should
Rechristen the place
From Shannontown to Bear City?
The Indians value most highly
Their claws & fat
Such proximity might profit my
Future citizens. At the villages of the Maha
We saw many regalia of bear claws
Larger than a man's fingers
Said to come from the Silver or Yellow Bear
Reputed fierce beyond measure—
The Indians do regard him as a fearful God
& Colter traded for one such necklace
To carry with him. Capt. Lewis anticipates

To find this gentleman
Farther up the Missouri & shoot some
For science & Pres. Jefferson.
If that bear is like to the black bear
As these grasshoppers is to ours
It must resemble more
A devil of a bear than a God of one.

Bear-Gods, Buffalo-Gods, Eagle-Gods—
Do such worthies hold sway
In these un-Christianized territories?
Do these little fellows wandering
Across my knuckles believe in some Ant-God
Of their own devising?
If we do not believe in Theirs
How should they believe
In One they have got no inkling of
& not their own kind & anyway
What purpose to carry on
About Ant-Gods, am I losing all sense?

Can the grass believe in God
Can the clouds—
Surely not. Might an ant?

If so I am well situated
To assume the role of Ant-God
& smush this rascal here into
A smudge
I wipe from my thumb
Glowering.

No other single ant takes notice
Of my divine judgment
But they busy themselves constantly with
Seeking & toil, seeking & toil.

Lucky I am not a jealous or a vengeful God
To feel the slight of their indifference.

I am the Ant-God.

Lo, I am the Ant-God
Worship me!

Perhaps I am playing
At Ant-Devil
Is rather more to the point?

I might conceive the Ant-Devil to resemble
That apparition in the grass there—
Skull of an antelope, it has
Such horns & rotted skin as to make one
Tremble in fear of such incarnation.
O but it is too tiny, the ant
Is too small to observe a skull entire
Just as I cannot conceive these plains
Beyond the miles I ride through
& the river bluffs northward
& the horizon which halts my vista
Of waving grasses to west & south.
The ant sees only the inch
It traverses, the ant knows only
The world of the ant
& does not imagine it
Other than his own—
Does not perceive it as such
I should say
For I doubt the ant
Capable of any grander conceptions.
The ant does not dream or imagine
Anything at all but is
A dutiful & worthy companion
Nonetheless.

Like a mighty nation in his industry
He scouts & wanders
From his hole in long streams
All seeking & toil.

               hole
                  ant
                    ant
                       seed
                    ant
                  ant
               ant
                  ant
                     dust
                          ant
                      ant
                        ant
                     ant
                  ant
                     skull
                          ant
                            ant
                      grass
                         dust
                      ant

```
                    ant

                ant

            ant

                ant

        ant

    hole
```

Upon reflection I do not believe
Any such Ant-God
To hold sway over these minute individuals
Nor the ant to be possessed
Of any mystical nature whatsoever.
He is a creature of laws
Orderly & warranted
In all actions by such directives.

You will comprehend my meaning
If you have seen them scout for food
& carry it back to their nest

Or if you have poured water upon their hill
To watch them work & scurry to halt the flood
Rolling back the grain of sand from the door
Each to its place, as a bucket brigade

Others building anew as an engineer of artillery
Devising his fortifications, trundling & hauling
Such materials, whilst others stand forth
As sentinels, or soldiers, or foragers
Gone to pry the dead wing from a damsel fly
Yet others clambering up & back down
To make report, legions underground
No doubt industriously digging new tunnels
Leading to new hills & doors beyond the flood
With no hint of lamentation or execration
Without prayer of any kind given forth.
Even so in the rain do they attend
To their business—well
It was no rain but I pissed
Upon their hill
Intending only a demonstration
Of their industry & hope
They will forgive a well-intended
Observer to their country.
The ant is a model citizen, all things considered.
They would be welcome as settlers
In Shannontown
If they could afford the mark-up.

If they were fat as beavers
I would love them better & eat them.

In fact I have already sampled some.
They are flavorless
& would not sustain me.

In truth I should be better off
Anyway as Mayor
Of the Ants than Ant-God.
See how I am transformed
From a believer
Into a Democrat & a Man of Science?

Having got beyond it nearly
I am little troubled by hunger now—
Having got so far into its grasp, I mean
That it beats upon me like a hollow drum.

I believe Constance Ebson a fine girl
Of whom my Mother would approve
& amply beautiful besides
Yet it would be a shame
To starve here
& forego marriage for this.
Lying with Constance in the hayloft
Echoes a bit like hunger

Though desire is a hunger one cannot die of.
The opposite of which
I have upon occasion sworn to her.
Forgive me, darling
I knew not whereof I spoke.

15.

I see now that I was set in my vanity

& blind to it as a stone

Cast into water. Surely the Capts. have passed on

To those Rocky Mountains & I suppose

I shall never see them or the Western Ocean

We set out to find. No doubt

They give me up

As captured by Indians, eaten by wolves

Drowned in the Missouri, &c.

The Corps of Discovery cannot wait

For one man lost upon the prairie, nor would

Pres. Jefferson approve it.

Nor is it their place to rest

& let the water

Come to them, they are pledged

To make their way to it

But being no longer any part of that company

& a free man alone

I may so rest, & choose to.

Rest & gird for what

May be.

I grow weak to frailty, what purpose

To continue? This black horse

Would feed me several days

In my extremity

& I might come to it yet

Though I would feel downcast

To kill what has caused such trouble to rescue

& that a mere postponement

Lest some canoe happen upon me soon

& what likelihood of that?

Vanity is what has got me

Into this.

Horses & bullets & vanity.

Better to loose the black horse

If it comes to it.

He might end snakebit

Or put to toil by the Sioux, yet I can imagine him

Living wild upon this prairie

After a fashion that might please Pres. Jefferson.

To have American horses

Run free here.

Why else send men forth

To survey & prospect its entry to the Union

& why charter the Capts. to scientific enquiry

Lest to enlarge both realms

Concurrently?

Such a hunter as myself
With game abounding to wither & starve
Seems unlucky.

Unkind.

I could wish for many things—
More balls in that shot pouch
Or more jerky taken from Drouillard
Or greater skill as a fisherman
Or salmon jumping into my hat
Or I don't know what.

When my brother John drowned in the Ohio River
The current snatched his body
Under & he was gone, one second to the next.
That was a rocky place
We knew better than to fish at
But we had once before
Caught a great sturgeon there, larger than a man
& we loved the chance
Of such again, being children.

Thomas & I searched two days
Alone for the body & some
Thought us drowned as well before we found him

Snagged up in willow branches
& carried him home on horseback.
Heavy to bear.
Mother took to bed with sadness
& Parson Macready a steady nurse to her
How else did we endure him
In our cabin?

Still I would abide by the river.

I find it less troublesome
Than the emptiness of these plains
Pressing so upon me.

Empty is one way to put it, another
That they are overfull
But not in keeping with a man.
Too large in both emptiness & fullness
Is what I mean to say.
I have a conception of my soul
Being taken up in their austerity & solitude
To be devoured
By the stars
& I mind it no longer.

My bones will weather as well
In prairie soil as any
& rest better unconsecrated.
What solace it might bring my Mother
To see me church-buried
Is over-mastered by the hypocrisy
Of enduring that unction.

I cannot believe the House of God
More fit to the task
Than this eternity of grass
Nor man nor beast
Would decline this tomb of clouds & wind
For a plain wood coffin
On some muddy hillside in Ohio.

If it is to dust we return
Best to proceed there directly
& more practical.

What weeds may rise through my ribcage
Shall feed some hungry elk or buffalo
As the ribs themselves supply a morsel
To the wolves. Who owns this land
More truly than the bones of the creatures

That layer & constitute it
Whatever the Law of man may say?

The last of the Maha will fade from the earth
Vanquished utterly by the Pawnee
& after the Pawnee the Sioux may perish
& eventually the Kentuckians & Ohioans &c—
I doubt not but my countrymen
Will populate in numbers these fulsome plains
But what untold count
Of years & men, of decades & centuries
What numberless generations will it require
Life by life & skeleton by skeleton
To claim this land from the buffalo?

Who finds this body
Be it known
My name is George Shannon
& I bequeath my remains
To seed this land
With American bones.

Lewis and Clark

*A cloudy morning. Set out very early. The river wide, &
shallow, crowded with sand bars. Passed the island on which we lay,
at one mile. Saw a village of barking squirrels, 970 yards long &
800 yards wide, situated on a gentle slope of a hill. Those animals
are numerous. I killed four, with a view to have their skins stuffed.*

*Here, the man who left us with the horses, 16 days ago,
George Shannon——he started 26th August, & has been ahead ever
since——joined us, nearly starved to death. He had been 12 days
without anything to eat but grapes & one rabbit, which he killed
by shooting a piece of hard stick in place of a ball. This man,
supposing the boat to be ahead, pushed on as long as he could.
When he became weak & feeble, determined to lay by & wait for
a trading boat, which is expected, keeping one horse for the last
recourse. Thus a man had like to have starved to death in a land of
plenty for the want of bullets or something to kill his meat.*

*We camped on the lee shore, above the mouth of a run. A hard
rain all the afternoon, & most of the night, with hard wind from
the N.W. I walked on shore the fore part of this day, over some
broken country, which continues about 3 miles back, & then is level
& rich——all plains. I saw several foxes, & killed an elk & 2 deer, &
squirrels. The men with me killed an elk, 2 deer, & a pelican.*

—WILLIAM CLARK,
CAPTAIN, CORPS OF DISCOVERY

AFTERWORD

———

GEORGE SHANNON was the youngest member of the Corps of Discovery, those remarkable frontiersmen signed on by Lewis and Clark for their great voyage of exploration. At best guess—the records are imprecise—he was born in 1785 in Claysville, Pennsylvania, making him seventeen or eighteen at the time they set forth, and still a teenager in the summer of 1804, when he became lost from his compatriots. He was, by all accounts, bright, cheerful and resourceful, a good singer, though not regarded as the best tracker or hunter of the group. His education outstripped almost all of the others, however, and he could converse with the Captains on a more equal footing than his peers. After his sixteen days wandering alone along the Missouri River, in what is now Nebraska and South Dakota, Shannon became lost one more time on the expedition—for three days, in present-day Wyoming—but again found his way back unharmed. Whatever combination of fecklessness and impetuosity got Shannon into these unique situations (no other member of the party got lost even once), it did nothing to lower the high esteem in which their youngest member was held by the Corps of Discovery, Lewis and Clark themselves included.

So high was that regard, that several years after the expedition William Clark proposed that Shannon and he go into business together as fur traders in St. Louis, under the name "George Shannon & Co." Shannon turned him down. His sights were set on a return home to the Ohio River valley, and a higher education. By this time, Shannon had already undertaken a second and less fortunate journey up the Missouri River, resulting in the loss of his leg, and very nearly of his life. That was in 1807, when a group of Lewis and Clark's former company were detailed to return Chief Shahaka to the Mandan tribe, sixteen hundred miles upriver. Shahaka had descended the Missouri with Lewis and Clark on their homeward voyage, in order to pay a visit to President Jefferson in Washington, and was in need of an escort to return to his tribe. Unfortunately, the party was ambushed by a group of Arikara Indians. Shannon was wounded in the battle, and his leg, grown gangrenous, later amputated in St. Charles, Missouri. Throughout the rest of his life he was known as "Peg-Leg" Shannon.

The loss of a single limb did little to slow "Peg-Leg" down. In 1808 he returned east, and enrolled at Transylvania University in Kentucky, the first college west of the Appalachians. In 1810 Clark sent him to Philadelphia to help Nicholas Biddle with the editing of Meriwether Lewis's journals, and while there Shannon undertook legal studies in hopes of becoming an army judge advocate. In the end, he returned to Kentucky, married into a Lexington family, allied himself with Henry Clay, and became a major player in the legal and political world there, serving several terms in the State House of Delegates before becoming a circuit court judge. He fathered seven children, and oversaw the education and training of three of his six younger brothers, David, James, and Wilson.

For two decades as a civic leader, Shannon cut a colorful figure—one tale has him throwing his wooden leg into a fire to win a drinking bet—and his career in Kentucky was eventful. Embroiled in the rough-and-tumble state politics of the day, Shannon was accused at various times of being a drunk and a gambler, as well as of letting political interests sway his judicial opinions. In his most dramatic moment, Shannon presided over the murder trial that produced a death sentence for the son of Kentucky's governor. Eventually, after the defeat of his political faction, and personal economic setbacks, Shannon picked up and moved west, settling in Missouri, where he served as state attorney, and ran unsuccessfully for the United States Senate against Thomas Hart Benton. He settled in St. Charles, the very town from which Lewis and Clark had officially commenced their ascent of the Missouri twenty-five years before, and where, afterward, his leg had been amputated. In the summer of 1836, Shannon traveled by horseback to try a murder case in Palmyra, Missouri, where he died suddenly, in court, on August 30th, at the age of fifty-one.

Three more Shannon brothers followed George's unlikely entry into politics: Thomas, a year younger, was a farmer and tobacco merchant who served many years in both the Ohio state senate and house of representatives, and one term as a United States congressman; James, after studying for the bar at his brother's law firm, married the daughter of Isaac Shelby, Kentucky's first governor. Appointed U.S. Charge d'Affaires in Central America in 1832, he died of yellow fever before reaching his post. Most remarkable of all is baby brother Wilson Shannon, born in 1802, as George prepared for his journey with Lewis and Clark.

Wilson served two terms as governor of Ohio (the first ever born in the state); in 1844 he resigned to take up an appointment as ambassador to Mexico, a post he occupied until diplomatic relations were broken off on the eve of the Mexican-American War. In 1849, Wilson led a group of Ohioans to California during the Gold Rush, and upon returning home was elected to the United States Congress. Finally, in 1855 Wilson was appointed governor of the Kansas Territory, in advance of its entry into the Union, just as the notorious violence between pro- and antislavery partisans reached its worst levels; he lasted a year, and was removed from his post with the territory in a virtual state of war.

The collective saga of the Shannon brothers composes a remarkable testament to the character of nineteenth-century America, and seems to cry out for documentation. Narrative poetry, I fear, is not up to the task, for which Melville, or perhaps Orson Welles, might qualify. Difficult as it is to resurrect the tenor of those times, the spirit of the Shannons, in its modern permutations, continues to make its mark upon American society.

Of the clan's patriarch, George Shannon Sr., little is known. He emigrated from the north of Ireland, married his fellow emigrant Mary Milligan, and was survived by nine remarkable children. Shortly after his namesake set forth with the Corps of Discovery, George Shannon Sr. was caught in a blizzard while deer hunting near his home in Belmont County, Ohio, and froze to death.

Young George Shannon was not among those who kept a journal on the Lewis and Clark expedition. He left no formal account of his sixteen-day odyssey on the prairie, and this is therefore not a historical but an imaginative document. It may be part coming of age adventure, part road trip, and part ironic quest narrative, but its wellspring rises from those vast, lonely spaces that continue to haunt the American consciousness, whether embodied in the landscape or housed within—for lack of a better word—the soul. George Shannon often got lost, but he always got found. May the same hold true for those who continue to follow in his footsteps, the majestic land he wandered, and the nation he was proud to call home.